THIS BOOK BELONGS TO

Madhusudan Lohia.
III O.

SBN   361 00422 2

Published by Purnell Books, a Division of
Macdonald & Co (Publishers) Ltd.,
Greater London House
Hampstead Road
London NW1 7QX
a BPCC plc Company
Reprinted 1986
Made and printed in Great Britain by
Purnell Book Production Ltd., Paulton, Bristol

MR. PLOD AND LITTLE NODDY

BY

Enid Blyton

CONTENTS

Macdonald Purnell

THE MILKMAN HEARD NODDY SINGING AS HE CAME
UP THE PATH

6

1. NODDY GOES SHOPPING

ONE morning when Noddy looked out of his window, his garden was so full of golden sunshine that he really *had* to sing a joyful song. Just listen to him!

"Oh what a lovely sunny day,
    It's spring again, it's spring!
The sun is shining bright and gay,
    It makes me want to sing!"

So he sang as he dressed himself, and he sang as he cooked his breakfast, and he jumped about for joy all the time. The sun looked in at his little window, and laughed to see him. Be careful, little Noddy, you'll drop your breakfast egg if you jump about like that!

The milkman heard him singing as he came up the path with Noddy's bottle of milk.

"That's a very nice song," he said. "You can have this little pot of cream if you'll allow me to sing your song as I go on my rounds."

"Oh yes, *of course*," said Noddy, beaming at him. "And you can tap my head three times if you like, and make it nod—it feels like nodding all the time this morning!"

So the milkman tapped Noddy's head three times and laughed to see it go nod-nid-nod at him.

Then off he went with his milk bottles, singing Noddy's little song. Everybody liked it, and soon all Toyland Village was singing it, even Mr. Plod the policeman. He was painting the outside of his police-station because it suddenly looked so dirty in the bright sunshine.

8

MR. PLOD WAS PAINTING THE OUTSIDE OF HIS
POLICE-STATION BECAUSE IT LOOKED SO DIRTY

There he is, look—singing loudly as he paints.

"Oh what a lovely sunny day,
It's spring again, it's spring!
The sun is shining bright and gay,
It makes me want to sing!"

Noddy went out to fetch his little car. It was jiggling up and down, longing to go out into the warm sun. It was very, very pleased to see Noddy.

"Parp-parp!" it said, joyfully. "PARP-PARP!"

Noddy drove carefully out of the garage, and then jumped out to polish his car with a duster. "You look as if you want a new coat of paint, little car," he said. "I really must see about it. Hallo—there's Mrs. Tubby Bear calling me. Coming, Mrs. Tubby!"

He ran to Mrs. Tubby Bear's gate, and up to the front door. "Hallo, little Noddy," she said. "I want you to do a little shopping for me, please."

"Right," said Noddy. "What is it you want?"

"Well, Mr. Tubby Bear is going to do some

house painting," said Mrs. Tubby Bear. "The sun is so bright today that it shows up all the dirty corners and the places where the paint is wearing off. Will you fetch me some tins of paint, Noddy, and two big paint-brushes? I've only half a tin left in my cupboard."

"Of course," said Noddy. "Is little Bruiny Bear going to do some painting too?"

"Certainly NOT!" said Mrs. Tubby. "He'd probably paint the chimneys yellow and blue— and he might even think it would be a good idea to paint your car bright green!"

"Oh NO!" said Noddy, in alarm. "Don't let Bruiny have a paint-brush, Mrs. Tubby Bear. Please don't."

"I shan't," said Mrs. Tubby Bear. "He painted my clothes-line last year— bright green—and then hung out my washing for me. Don't you remember—all my sheets were striped with green paint when I went to fetch them!"

"Where *is* Bruiny?" asked Noddy. "He borrowed

my little stool yesterday and he hasn't brought it back."

"He's gone to buy some lollipops," said Mrs. Tubby Bear. "I'll tell him to give you your stool as soon as he comes back."

Mrs. Tubby Bear gave Noddy a list of the paints she wanted, and he nodded his head. "Right. I'll bring them all back as soon as I can—and the paint-brushes too."

Off he went in his little car with the list—parp-parp! The car jiggled about joyfully as it went, it really was *such* a lovely day!

Noddy suddenly saw Bruiny Bear coming along sucking a lollipop. He stopped and shouted to him.

"Hey, Bruiny Bear—just you return my little red stool to me, see? I want it. And what about giving me a lollipop for lending you my stool?"

"I can't spare one," said Bruiny, and walked off on his fat little legs. He licked his lollipop as he went, although his mother had told him he must NOT suck lollipops when he was out in the street.

Noddy went to the paint-shop. It was piled with tins from floor to ceiling. Noddy thought they looked nice. He felt as if *he* wanted to buy some tins of paint too.

"I could paint my garage doors," he thought. "I could paint my front door too. Wouldn't Big-Ears be surprised! I might even paint my little car!"

He bought the tins that Mrs. Tubby Bear wanted, and stacked them into his car. He bought a few for himself too. It really would be fun to paint!

Then away he went through the village, parp-parp-parp-parp, the tins jiggling merrily. Noddy sang a little song to them:

> "Rattle and shake,
> What a noise you make,
> Tins at the back of the car
> Jiggle and jump
> And bumpetty bump—
> What fidgety tins you are!"

2. MR. PLOD DOES SOME PAINTING

THE tins at the back of his car rattled and
shook happily while Noddy sang, and everyone
turned to see what the noise was. Noddy waved
and smiled, he felt so happy. He slowed down
a little at the cross-roads, for he was sure Mr.
Plod would shout at him for going too fast.

But Mr. Plod wasn't there! Noddy was surprised.
"Where's Mr. Plod?" he shouted to the Wobbly-
Man who was on the pavement nearby, talking to
Mickey Monkey.

"Painting the outside of the police-station!" shouted back Mr. Wobbly-Man.

"He's high up on the ladder!" called Mickey Monkey. "And I hope he falls off!"

"That's a *bad* thing to say," said the Wobbly-Man, frowning at Mickey Monkey.

"Well, if he falls off, nobody will be scolded or locked up or smacked," said Mickey Monkey. "I don't like Mr. Plod."

"That's because you're a bad monkey," said the Wobbly-Man. "It's a very good thing we've a policeman to look after us all, and see that we aren't robbed at night. Isn't it, Noddy? My word—what a lot of painting you're going to do!"

"Oh—the tins are mostly for Mrs. Tubby Bear," said Noddy, nodding his head. "Only a few are mine. I thought I'd paint my garage doors."

"Wonderful idea!" said Mickey Monkey at once. "I'll help you, Noddy."

"No you won't," said Noddy at once. "And if you dare to come prying round my little House-For-One, do you know what I'll do? I'll paint your hair green!"

And off he went at top speed. He thought he would go past the police-station and see how Mr. Plod was getting on with his painting. Good gracious—what a long ladder he had, stretching all the way up to the roof!

"He's right at the top," thought Noddy. "Goodness, I hope he doesn't fall—he *would* get a bump! And who's that at the bottom, holding the ladder? Hurrah, it's Big-Ears! Hey, Big-Ears, parp-parp-PARP!"

Big-Ears jumped when he heard the loud tooting, and looked round crossly.

"Oh—it's you, Noddy. You made me jump so much that I nearly let go the ladder! Please don't do things like that!"

17

Noddy hoped that Mr. Plod
wouldn't fall down the ladder on
top of poor Big-Ears. He shouted
up to Mr. Plod:

"Be careful, Mr. Plod,
  The ladder's very tall,
  And Big-Ears is so small
  That if you slip and fall
  You'll SQUASH him, Mr. Plod!"

But Mr. Plod didn't hear him.

He looked down at Noddy and shouted to him.
"I hope you're being good! You've no idea how
far I can see when I stand on this high ladder.
I can keep a watch on nearly everyone as I paint."

Noddy felt alarmed. "Can you see my little
house from the top of your ladder?" he asked.

"Oh yes," said Mr. Plod. "I can
see the Tubby Bears' house too—and
I can even see Bruiny Bear going up
to your front door."

"What's he going there for?" said
Noddy, frowning. "Oh—maybe he's
taking back my stool."

"He's certainly carrying some-
thing," said Mr. Plod. "And, dear me, I can
see little Tessie Bear with her shopping-basket.

"I CAN SEE THE TUBBY BEARS' HOUSE—AND I CAN
EVEN SEE BRUINY BEAR GOING TO YOUR FRONT
DOOR," SAID MR. PLOD

19

She's going to your house too, I think, Noddy, with Bumpy-Dog—yes, she's stopped to talk to Bruiny."

"What are they talking about?" asked Noddy.

"Now how *can* Mr. Plod hear their talk all this way away?" said Big-Ears. "You'd better go back home, Noddy, and give Tessie Bear some lemonade. I'll come and see you soon. I'm thinking of painting my Toadstool House, and I might want you to fetch *me* some tins of paint."

"Right, Big-Ears," said Noddy. "You just let me know. I might help you." And away he went at top speed, not hearing Mr. Plod shouting at him from the top of the ladder, ordering him not to go so fast!

"I hope Tessie Bear is still at my house," he thought. "And I hope Bumpy-Dog is behaving himself and not digging up half my garden."

Tessie Bear was waiting at the gate for him, holding Bumpy-Dog's collar. "Hallo, Noddy," she said, smiling all over her little furry face.

20

"I've brought you a chocolate cake. I made it myself."

"You *are* clever, Tessie!" said Noddy, jumping out of his car and giving Tessie a hug. The Bumpy-Dog at once leapt up to kiss him too, and poor Noddy sat down hard on the path, with Bumpy-Dog on top of him.

"Go away, Bumpy-Dog!" he shouted. "Get off my tummy!"

"Parp-parp!" said Noddy's little car, very fiercely indeed. It frightened Bumpy-Dog so much that he left Noddy and ran to hide under a bush.

"Thank you, little car," said Noddy, getting up. "Hoot like that again if Bumpy-Dog comes after me. And just you listen to *me*, Bumpy! There's NO bone buried in my garden, so don't dare dig a hole anywhere!"

He went indoors with Tessie. The first thing he saw was his little red stool. "Oh good!" he said. "You have the chair, Tessie, and I'll have the stool. Shall we each have a slice of chocolate cake—and some lemonade?"

"Yes, please," said Tessie—and soon she was in the chair eating a big slice of the lovely chocolate cake she had made, and Noddy was on the stool, enjoying it too.

"It's LOVELY, Tessie," he said—and then stopped in alarm. His car was hooting again— parp-parp, parp-PARP! What was happening? Was Bumpy-Dog digging up his garden, looking for a bone that wasn't there?

"He wants a SMACKING!" said Noddy, looking very fierce, and jumped up from the stool. "I'll go and see what's happening!"

3. A FEW SURPRISES

NODDY rushed out into the garden—yes, Bumpy-Dog *was* digging a hole. Noddy rushed at him, shouting so loudly that Bumpy was surprised. He leapt right over the fence and landed in Mrs. Tubby Bear's garden.

"All right—you stay there!" said Noddy, crossly. "But let me warn you, you'll be very sorry if Mr. Tubby Bear catches you digging holes in *his* garden!"

He turned to go back and saw Gilbert Golly and Sailor Doll looking over his gate. They began to laugh loudly and pointed to him.

"What's the matter?" said Noddy, in surprise.

"Look behind you," said Sailor Doll. Noddy

TESSIE BEGAN TO LAUGH TOO! NODDY STARED
AT HER IN SURPRISE

looked behind him, but all he could see was a clump of primroses growing in a corner. Sailor Doll and Gilbert Golly pointed to him again, and rolled about, laughing.

"Well, laugh all you like," said Noddy. "I looked behind me and all I could see were those primroses—and if you want to laugh at *them*, well, laugh!"

He went indoors, quite cross. But good gracious, as soon as he walked into the room, Tessie began to laugh, too! Noddy stared at her in surprise.

"What's the matter?" he said.

"Look behind you," said Tessie Bear, giggling.

"I've already done that," said Noddy, looking behind him again. "I can see that little table— but it isn't a *funny* table. It doesn't make me want to laugh. The primroses weren't funny, either."

"Stand in front of the mirror and look behind you," said Tessie.

Noddy went to the mirror, stood with his back

25

to it and then looked behind him, into the glass. And what a surprise he had! His little shorts were bright red at the back, instead of blue!

"Who's painted them red?" he shouted. "Who..." And then he guessed what had happened.

"It's that horrid Bruiny Bear! He's re-painted my stool red, look—and I sat down on the wet paint, so I'm all red at the back! Oh, TESSIE, I'll paint Bruiny's tail green, I'll . . ."

"He hasn't any tail," said Tessie, with another giggle.

"Well, I'll paint his ears blue, and I'll pull his . . ." began Noddy, in a great temper, and then stopped suddenly. Bumpy-Dog had just appeared at the open door, wagging his tail, his tongue hanging out, asking to come in.

But what a PECULIAR Bumpy-Dog! His ears were red. His tail was red. He had big round red

26

spots all over his body! He looked simply dreadful.

Tessie Bear burst into tears. "Oh, poor Bumpy!" she sobbed. "Look, Noddy—that horrid Bruiny has painted Bumpy-Dog too. Go away, Bumpy— you will rub red paint all over me. Oh, Bumpy, how *could* you let Bruiny do that to you?"

"Wuff!" said Bumpy, putting his tail down. He was very sad. He had thought that he looked really lovely. Poor Bumpy.

Noddy stared at Bumpy-Dog—and then, oh dear, he began to laugh! How he laughed! Bumpy went into a corner and sat down, looking at Noddy very sadly. He hated being laughed at.

"You're unkind to laugh, Noddy," said Tessie,

wiping her eyes. "Bumpy will be very unhappy—
everyone will laugh at him. I'll have to give him
at least three baths before I can rub the paint
off his coat."

"Wuff!" said Bumpy, in alarm. One bath was
bad enough—but THREE would be dreadful. He
ran suddenly to the window and jumped out of it,
landing right on top of the primroses. Oh *dear*!

Then all at once there was a very loud noise
outside. Bumpy-Dog was barking in excitement
and someone was shouting in surprise.

"Bumpy-Dog! What's happened to you? You've
a red tail and red ears! Where's Noddy? I must
find him quickly. It's very important."

"Why—that's Big-Ears' voice!" cried Noddy,
running to the door. "Big-Ears—what's the matter? You sound worried. Whatever's happened?"

4. POOR MR. PLOD

BIG-EARS came into Noddy's house, looking very hot and bothered. He had left his bicycle by the gate.

"Noddy! I'm so glad you're at home! Who was that dog I saw just now—with red ears and tail and spots? What a terrible-looking creature! I nearly turned and ran!"

"It was only Bumpy-Dog," said Noddy. "Bruiny's painted him all over with some old red paint his mother had. Big-Ears, what's the matter? You do look scared."

"I am," said Big-Ears, taking out an enormous hanky and mopping his head. "Mr. Plod fell off that ladder, Noddy—right from the top to the bottom—BUMP!"

"Good *gracious*!" said Noddy, in alarm. "Is he hurt?"

"I don't know," said Big-Ears. "He'll have to go to the hospital and see the doctor. Will you take him there in your car? It's very important."

"Of course I will!" said Noddy. "Oh, *poor* Mr. Plod! I hope he hasn't broken himself anywhere. I'll get my car, Big-Ears, and we'll go to the police-station at once. Does anyone else know?"

"Oh yes—everybody," said Big-Ears. "And I'm sorry to say that Gilbert Golly and Bruiny Bear and Mickey Monkey, and a few others aren't very sorry."

"Well—I'm VERY VERY sorry," said Noddy. "Mr. Plod is cross with me sometimes, but I do like him, Big-Ears, and I think he's a good policeman. I'm SO sorry he's fallen off his ladder. I'll take him to hospital at once in my car."

"Who will be policeman now?" asked Tessie, her eyes full of tears because she was so upset about Mr. Plod.

"*I* shall," said Big-Ears, in such a stern voice

NODDY DROVE MR. PLOD VERY, VERY CAREFULLY
TO THE HOSPITAL

31

that Noddy felt quite afraid. "So just you behave yourselves, Tessie and Noddy."

Noddy ran to get his car, and soon he and Big-Ears were speeding through the village. In no time at all poor Mr. Plod was gently lifted into the car, and Noddy drove him very very carefully to the hospital.

Noddy didn't much like the hospital. He was afraid of the doctors and the nurses. He was afraid

he might be put to bed there, and have medicine to drink. Poor Mr. Plod—would he be very unhappy there?

Mr. Plod was very brave. Noddy thought he was wonderful. He didn't groan or grumble or sigh. All he said was that he was sorry, very sorry, about one thing.

"What's that?" asked Noddy.

"It's my helmet," said Mr. Plod. "It was dreadfully dented. I'm worried about that. Very worried. Big-Ears, I hope you'll see what can be done about that."

They left poor Mr. Plod at the dear little white hospital, in charge of a kind-looking doctor and two nurses. "Come and see me tomorrow," said Mr. Plod to Big-Ears. "I'll be lonely and sad. And be a good policeman, Big-Ears."

Then he was put in a wheel-chair and taken away. Noddy began to cry.

"What's hospital like?" he said. "I don't like it."

"We'll soon see,' said Big-Ears. "We'll visit Mr. Plod tomorrow, and take him some flowers."

"And some toffee. He likes that," said Noddy, driving his car away. "And I'll take him some of Tessie's chocolate cake."

"I might take him some apples," said Big-Ears. "Hey, Noddy—where are you going? I want to go to the police-station, not to Toadstool House!"

So Noddy drove Big-Ears to the police-station—and dear me, when Big-Ears had put on Mr. Plod's spare helmet, and sat up on his high stool, he really looked rather alarming.

"I don't like you in that helmet," said Noddy. "You look as though you want to lock me up or something. Big-Ears, you will be a *kind* police-man, won't you?"

"I shall be kind to good people but I shall be very *FIERCE* with bad ones," said Big-Ears. "So just you be good, little Noddy!"

34

5. MR. PLOD IS VERY HAPPY

WELL, the news soon went round Toyland Village that Mr. Plod had fallen off his ladder and gone into hospital. What a to-do there was!

"Who is going to protect us against robbers?" said Miss Fluffy Cat.

"Who is going to direct the traffic and see that cars don't go too fast?" said the Wobbly-Man.

"Who is going to stop Mickey Monkey and his friends from being rude to people and making faces at them?" said Miss Kitten.

"I AM!" said Big-Ears, in a very deep voice. And, dear me, there he was next day at the cross-roads, helmet on head, directing the traffic —and HOW cross he was with Gilbert Golly for riding his bicycle too fast! He made him hold out his hand for a good smack with Mr. Plod's truncheon.

Noddy took Tessie Bear to see Mr. Plod while Big-Ears was busy. They took flowers and half the chocolate cake and toffee and a book to read.

They felt scared when they came to the white hospital. A nurse met them and smiled, and said, "Oh, it is that nice Mr. Plod you want, is it? Come along—he's had quite a lot of visitors already."

"Is he better? Is he very sad?" asked Tessie.

"He's feeling much better," said the nurse, who looked very kind and pretty. "And, goodness me, he's not feeling at ALL sad! Why should he? Hospital is a lovely place to be in. Just wait till you see him!"

And then she took them into a big room with

"MR. PLOD, YOU DO LOOK WELL AND HAPPY,"
SAID NODDY. "I'M SO GLAD"

lots of beds—and in one of them was Mr. Plod sitting up, looking very happy indeed. Flowers were on a table beside him, a box of chocolates, five new books, his favourite cigarettes, and a bottle of lemonade! He was even wearing a nice paper helmet that kind Mrs. Tubby Bear had sent him. Bruiny Bear had had it in a Christmas cracker!

"Hallo, hallo!" he said to Noddy and Tessie. "How are you? Goodness, are those flowers for me—and this LOVELY chocolate cake—and these toffees—and what an exciting book! I only hope I'll be in hospital long enough to read it all through. Sit down. How is Big-Ears getting on?"

"Mr. Plod, you do look well and happy," said Noddy. "I'm so glad."

"Well, that's what you come to hospital for, isn't it?" said Mr. Plod. "To be made well and happy. I've never had such a good time in my life. It seems as if EVERYbody loves me—even that scamp Bruiny Bear! He brought me three lollipops this morning! Oh, I *am* enjoying myself!"

"But didn't you hurt yourself when you fell off the ladder?" asked Noddy.

38

"Oh yes, it hurt at the time," said Mr. Plod. "But those kind nurses and the doctors bathed and bandaged me, and then put lovely ointment on my bruises, and fussed over me—and really I feel quite all right again. I tell you, hospital is a LOVELY place to come to. I can't *imagine* why some silly people are afraid of going there. It's as good as a holiday—better, because everybody gives you presents."

"Well—if ever *I* was ill or had an accident, I'd LOVE to go to hospital," said Tessie Bear.

"Yes. So would I," said Noddy. "Fancy having kind visitors and lovely presents, and never being scolded, and no work to bother about. Everybody in bed here seems to have flowers beside them, and little presents."

"You tell Big-Ears I'm going to stay here as long as I can," said Mr. Plod. "It's the nicest place I've ever been in. Ah—here comes another

visitor—the dear Wobbly-Man. Look what he's brought me—a great big box of sweets!"

Noddy and Tessie slipped away. Well, well—to think they had felt sorry for poor Mr. Plod being in hospital—and there he was, in a lovely cosy bed, with lots of people to talk to all round him, and so many visitors with presents that really he would soon have to have another table beside him to carry them all!

"Could you make up a Hospital Song, Noddy?" said Tessie Bear. "One that will tell everyone what a lovely place a hospital is? Then nobody would mind going there. Make up a song, Noddy, do—and sing it to everyone who asks you about Mr. Plod and the hospital!"

"Right!" said Noddy. "I can feel one coming into my head. Look—there's Sally Skittle and her children waving to me. I expect they'll ask me about Mr. Plod—so I'll be able to sing them my Hospital Song!"

Sure enough Sally Skittle did ask him. "How is poor, poor Mr. Plod in hospital?" she said. "It must be dreadful to be taken there!"

"COULD YOU MAKE UP A HOSPITAL SONG, NODDY?" SAID
TESSIE BEAR. "ONE THAT WILL TELL EVERYONE WHAT
A LOVELY PLACE A HOSPITAL IS?"

41

"Oh, he's *fine*," said Noddy. "And very very happy. He says it's just like a lovely holiday. Let me sing you my Hospital Song, Sally Skittle, and you listen too, all you Skittle children, and you'll never, never mind going to hospital if ever you have to!"

And Noddy raised his voice and sang loudly.

"If ever I'm hurt or sick or ill,
  I would simply LOVE to go
And stay in a hospital bright and gay,
  With little beds all in a row!
I'd love all the nurses who fuss around,
  I'd love all my visitors too,
And the beautiful flowers and gifts they bring,
  I'd be happy the whole day through!

42

So if ever *you're* ill, and you have to go,
Don't pull a very long face,
But say 'What a treat—at last I will see
This happy and wonderful place'!"

"Well, that's a good song to hear," said Sally Skittle, and she beamed round at all her Skittle children. "Now just remember little ones—if ever *you* have to go to hospital, go with a great big smile!"

What a nice song, Noddy. We do like it very much—and Tessie Bear likes it most of all!

6. BIG-EARS FEELS WORRIED

BIG-EARS was a very, very good policeman. He didn't wear Mr. Plod's uniform because it was much too big for him, but he did wear Mr. Plod's spare helmet, and he had Mr. Plod's truncheon too.

"I've sent Mr. Plod's dented helmet to be mended," he told Noddy, as Noddy stopped his car in the village street, where Big-Ears was watching the traffic. "I'm glad he's getting on so well. He's been in hospital three days now, and isn't he loving it!"

"I hope he won't mind leaving it," said Noddy. "He's having such a lovely time there! Big-Ears, you look a bit worried. Is anything the matter?"

"Well, yes—I do feel a bit worried," said Big-Ears. "Somebody broke into the Wobbly-Man's house last night and stole a lot of money. And

44

this morning Mr. Golly at the garage told me that two bicycles had been stolen from one of his sheds."

"Good gracious! Who stole them?" said Noddy, in surprise. "Just when Mr. Plod is in hospital too!"

"Yes—and I'm so afraid that if he gets to hear

of these robberies he will jump out of bed and come hurrying home to try and find the thieves!" said Big-Ears. "And I don't see how I can leave my post here and go hunting for robbers. I don't know what to do!"

"I'll see what *I* can do," said little Noddy, bravely. "I'll go and ask Mr. Golly to tell me all he knows about the stealing of the bicycles. There must be *two* thieves to steal two bicycles, don't you think that's right, Big-Ears?"

"Yes," said Big-Ears, looking sternly at the clockwork clown, who was going head-over-heels across the road instead of walking.

Noddy drove off to Mr. Golly's garage. He liked kind Mr. Golly. He had some petrol put into his car, and asked Mr. Golly about the robbers who had taken the bicycles.

"They came into this shed," said Mr. Golly, showing Noddy a little shed. "The door was locked, so they came in at that skylight window in the roof."

Noddy stood on a chair and looked carefully at the skylight. He saw something on the edge of the skylight—what was it? He rubbed it off with his finger and looked at it.

"Hairs!" he said. "Look, Mr. Golly—brown

hairs! Whoever came in there was a *furry* toy—some of his hairs rubbed off on the skylight as he squeezed through."

"The robbers must have been very clever," said Mr. Golly. "They must have passed the bicycles up through the skylight, climbed over the roof with them, and then down to the ground. Now what toys could possibly do that?"

"Monkeys could," said Noddy, nodding his head. "They can climb anywhere. And I'm sure that's monkey-fur left on the edge of the skylight."

"Well—they'll never be caught, I'm afraid," said Mr. Golly. "You know they took the Wobbly-Man's money too? And I hear that they must have been to Miss Fluffy Cat's and taken her lovely necklace."

"I'm going to find those thieves!" said Noddy, fiercely, and he ran out to his car. He drove up to the hospital to see Mr. Plod, and took him a very large sweet orange. And, oh dear, what a pity— Mr. Plod had heard of the robbers, and wanted to get up at once and go back to the police-station.

"Big-Ears will *never* catch them!" he said to Noddy. "They're too clever! I must get up and go back to my job. I must catch those thieves before they rob any more people. Fetch my clothes for me, Noddy—they're in that cupboard there!"

"Now, now, Mr. Plod—you mustn't be naughty," said a nice little nurse. "Your head and your bruises aren't quite mended yet, you know."

"Mr. Plod—I'LL catch those robbers for you," said Noddy. "Don't you worry. *I'll* get them!"

And away he went in his little car. Now— where had those two nasty robbers gone?

7. NODDY IS BRAVE AND CLEVER

NODDY went back to Mr. Golly's shop. He went round to the bicycle shed, and had a good look around. It had been raining in the night, and Noddy could quite plainly see the marks of two bicycles in the mud outside the shed.

"Ha! Those monkeys hopped on to the bicycles just here—and rode off up the lane behind the garage!" said Noddy, in excitement. "I can see the tracks quite plainly. I'll follow them!"

So away he went in his car, following the muddy tracks—up the lane, round a corner, across a field, and up another lane into a little wood. His car couldn't go through the wood, because there was no path to follow. So Noddy jumped

"THIS IS SILLY!" SAID NODDY TO HIMSELF. "BICYCLES
DON'T SUDDENLY DISAPPEAR INTO THE AIR"

out, and followed the bicycle tracks on foot.

Well, what a strange thing! The tracks came to a very sudden end indeed at the foot of a big old tree! Noddy went all round the tree but he couldn't see any more bicycle tracks at all!

"This is silly!" said Noddy to himself. "Bicycles don't suddenly disappear into the air. And there aren't any footprints either."

Then he suddenly heard a peculiar noise. "It's like the farmer's old pig, grunting away!" thought Noddy. "And it's coming from above my head, up this old tree!"

He looked up into the tree—and WHAT a surprise he had! Two bicycles were hanging there in the branches—and two sleeping monkeys were cuddled together in a hole in the trunk—and how loudly they were snoring!

"No wonder they sleep all day if they go round robbing people all night!" thought Noddy. "Now—what am I to do? I can't get the bicycles without waking them—and I certainly can't fight two monkeys at once!"

And then he saw something that made him feel very pleased. Each monkey had a key in his back—a big key, sticking out. "*Clockwork* monkeys!" thought Noddy. "They have keys to wind them up, just like clockwork clowns. If ONLY I could take those keys, they wouldn't be able to chase me far—their clockwork would run down!"

Climb up carefully, Noddy—that's right. Lower that bicycle down—sh—don't make a noise! Now the other one—clever little Noddy! Those wicked little monkeys are still fast asleep!

Now climb up again and see if you can take the keys—carefully now—oh, you nearly slipped on that branch! Now—reach out and take the first monkey's key—good, good, good! Now the second one's—it's a bit stiff, but you've managed it, Noddy. Hurrah! Slip down the tree, and put the bicycles into the back of your car.

Noddy, the monkeys have heard you! They are awake—they're shouting—they're climbing down the tree—oh, do hurry! They're after you, Noddy,

they're after you! *Please* hurry, Noddy!

But Noddy doesn't mind. He knows quite well that their clockwork will soon run down, and they will have to stop and lie down until somebody winds them up again. And he has their keys! Clever little Noddy!

Away he goes, with the bicycles bumping at the back, singing a loud and happy song! Listen to him.

"Oh what do you think? I found the thieves
  Up in a tree, among the leaves;
  I found the bicycles up there too,
  They're here in my car, yes, it's REALLY true!
  And I've taken the keys of the thieves as well,
  No wonder I'm nodding, and ringing my bell!
  I don't really mind if they chase me fast,
  Their clockwork is sure to run down at last,
  And then they'll be caught, and Big-Ears will say,
  'Well done, Little Noddy, and hip-hip hurray!' "

And now Noddy has come to Toyland Village, driving at top speed to tell Big-Ears what has happened. Big-Ears is cross to see him driving so fast.

"Stop, Noddy, stop! You've no right to be going so fast!" he shouts. And Noddy stops just by him, grinning all over his happy face, his head nodding away fast.

"I've found the stolen bicycles, Big-Ears—and I've taken away the keys of the two monkey-robbers! Their clockwork will soon run down, so they'll fall over and lie still—and we can easily catch them! Oh, Big-Ears—I've had SUCH an adventure!"

8. A SURPRISE FOR NODDY!

WHAT an excitement there was when the news spread round! Big-Ears sent Mr. Tubby Bear, Mr. Golly from the garage, and Mr. Wobbly-Man to catch the two monkeys. They found them lying quite still under a tree, very angry indeed because their keys had gone, and they couldn't run any further.

"You come along with *us*!" said Mr. Tubby, very sternly. "I shall lock you up, and I shouldn't be surprised if Big-Ears doesn't give you a good whipping—stealing bicycles and money, and running off like that!"

Big-Ears was very pleased to lock up the two bad monkeys. "Now Mr. Plod won't think he must leave hospital and come and catch you," he said.

Mr. Plod was certainly very very pleased when Big-Ears told him the news. He lay back in bed and gave a happy sigh. "Well, that's fine!" he

said. "Now I can stay in this lovely hospital a bit longer. Good little Noddy—he really ought to have a reward, Big-Ears."

"Well, I've thought of one," said Big-Ears. "Noddy has bought some paint to paint his front door, Mr. Plod—but really he's not very good at painting, you know. What about paying Mr. Bear, Tessie Bear's uncle, to do the painting—he's a very good painter."

"A splendid idea!" said Mr. Plod, pleased. "Fancy Noddy catching those two thieves—you know, he's very naughty sometimes, Big-Ears, but he's very very good at heart, isn't he?"

And Big-Ears nodded his head up and down just like Noddy, and said "YES, YES, YES" very loudly indeed. "We'll give a party for you when you come out of hospital, Mr. Plod," he said. "We SHALL be glad to have you back."

He went to ask Mr. Bear, Tessie's uncle, to paint Noddy's garage and front-door for him.

Mr. Bear was delighted for he loved painting.

"Certainly, certainly!" he said. "And if you can manage to let me have his car for a day, I will paint that too! Good little fellow, Noddy. Don't tell him anything about this. It shall be a real surprise."

Tessie Bear was very excited to hear what was going to be done for Noddy. "*I* know how we can get him out of the way for a whole day," she said. "I'll ask him to catch the Toyland Train with me and go to my Granma Bear for a whole day. She lives in Teddy-Bear Town, so Noddy will be right out of the way when the painting is done!"

And that is just what Tessie did—she took Noddy off to Teddy-Bear Town in the train—and all that day Mr. Bear, her uncle, painted away, down at Noddy's house, and Mr. Tubby Bear helped as well. Bruiny wanted to help too, but they did not trust him.

"No—you'd paint red spots on Noddy's front door or do something silly, just like you did with the poor Bumpy-Dog!" said Mr. Tubby. "Tessie couldn't wash off his red spots, and he still looks very peculiar. Go away before I paint your nose green!"

When Noddy came back with Tessie from Teddy-Bear Town he couldn't believe his eyes! His front door was a beautiful new green—his garage was shining yellow—and you should have seen his car! It had never, never looked so grand before. Noddy stood looking at it, his head nodding up and down in joy, his eyes as big as saucers!

"My little car—it looks as good as new! And the garage—it's beautiful—and my front door! Who's done all this, and why?"

"It's a little reward for you, Noddy," said

Mr. Tubby. "You caught those robbers, you know, and that meant that Mr. Plod didn't have to get up and walk out of the hospital before he was well. You *deserve* a reward, Noddy."

"Hurrah!" shouted everyone, and the little car joined in too, with a very loud "PARP PARP PARP!" The Bumpy-Dog rushed up, barking, and jumped at Noddy to lick him—and, oh dear, down he went, of course!

But Noddy was too happy to scold Bumpy. He hugged Tessie, he hugged Big-Ears, he hugged Mr. Tubby and Mrs. Tubby, and, quite by mistake, he hugged naughty little Bruiny, too! What a joyful time that was.

Noddy couldn't help singing, of course! And what a happy song it was! Listen.

" Oh, I do feel so happy today, today,
For I AM so lucky, you see,
I've a dear little house, and a garage too,
And friends that are fond of me.
I've a beautiful car with a loud parp-parp,
And *plenty* of room inside
To take the people of Toyland Town
Wherever they want to ride.
I love Mrs. Tubby, and Tessie Bear too,
And Big-Ears, my Very Best Friend,
I'm really so happy I *might* sing all day—
But I think my song's come to an end!"

You make us feel happy too, little Noddy!
Goodbye, till we see you again.